This edition published by Parragon Books Ltd in 2017

Parragon Books Ltd
Chartist House
15–17 Trim Street
Bath BA1 1HA, UK
www.parragon.com

ISBN 978-1-4748-9266-7

Printed in China

DISNEY PRINCESS

Tangled

Magical
Story

PaRRagon

Bath • New York • Cologne • Melbourne • Delhi
Hong Kong • Shenzhen • Singapore

Once upon a time, a drop of sunlight fell to Earth and it grew into a magical golden flower that had healing powers.

Centuries later, the Queen of a nearby kingdom fell ill. The townspeople found the healing flower. The Queen got better and soon after she gave birth to a baby girl who she called Rapunzel.

One night, a selfish old woman called Mother Gothel discovered that the flower's power had gone into Rapunzel's hair, so she snatched Rapunzel from the castle and vanished. Mother Gothel wanted to use the hair to stay eternally young.

Mother Gothel locked Rapunzel in a tower and raised her as her own daughter, but she only loved Rapunzel for her magic hair.

Each year on Rapunzel's birthday, the kingdom lit lanterns to help their lost princess find her way home.

"Can I go to see the floating lights?" Rapunzel asked the day before her eighteenth birthday.

But Mother Gothel told Rapunzel that the outside world was too cruel and dangerous.

Meanwhile, a thief called Flynn was on the run with his partners in crime, the Stabbington brothers. He clutched a satchel that held a stolen royal crown! Flynn was afraid of the Stabbingtons, so he ran off with the satchel.

But the Captain of the Guard and his horse, Maximus, were on his heels! Flynn knocked the Captain off and took the reins. Maximus sank his teeth into the satchel.

As Flynn yanked the satchel free, it went flying into the air.

The satchel hooked onto a tree overhanging a cliff. As Flynn and Maximus fought, they fell into a canyon.

Flynn ran off with the satchel and stumbled through a dark tunnel into a hidden valley. He looked up and saw a tower in the distance – it would make the perfect hiding place!

He climbed up the tower and into an open window.

CLANG! Suddenly, everything went black.

Rapunzel had sneaked up behind Flynn and knocked him out with a frying pan! Although Flynn didn't look like the scary men Mother Gothel had warned her about, Rapunzel hid him in a cupboard – she was worried Mother Gothel would return.

Then, Rapunzel noticed the crown in Flynn's satchel. She put it on her head and gazed into the mirror. She felt different somehow.

Suddenly, Mother Gothel came back. Rapunzel asked to see the floating lights again.

"You are not leaving this tower! EVER!" roared
Mother Gothel.

So Rapunzel asked for special paint that required
Mother Gothel to go on a three-day journey.

As soon as she left, Rapunzel dragged Flynn out of
the cupboard, tied him up
and offered him a deal.
If he took her to see
the floating lights,
she would give him
the satchel.

Flynn agreed.

Rapunzel longed to leave the tower, but she was also terrified. She had never been outside before!
With her pet chameleon, Pascal, on her shoulder, Rapunzel slid down her hair.

Rapunzel was having the time of her life, but she also felt terrible for betraying Mother Gothel.

Flynn tried to take advantage by making Rapunzel feel worse.

"Does your mother deserve this?" he asked. "I'm letting you out of the deal. Let's turn round and get you home."

But Rapunzel insisted. "I'm seeing those lanterns."

Not far from the tower, Mother Gothel found Maximus.
Worried the palace guards had found Rapunzel, she
raced back.

Mother Gothel searched everywhere, but Rapunzel was
gone. Then she spotted the crown and Flynn's WANTED
poster. Now she knew exactly who had taken Rapunzel
and she was going to find him!

Flynn led Rapunzel to a pub filled with scary-looking thugs. He was hoping to frighten Rapunzel into returning to the tower. Then Maximus, the royal guards and the captive Stabbington brothers burst in. Flynn, Rapunzel and Pascal escaped through a secret passageway.

Flynn and Rapunzel hid in a cavern, but it started to flood with water. Flynn cut his hand on jagged rocks.

"This is all my fault," Rapunzel said tearfully. "I'm so sorry."

Then Rapunzel revealed her secret: "Flynn, I have magic hair that glows when I sing."

Suddenly, she realized her hair could glow and show them the way out!

Mother Gothel found the Stabbington brothers and offered them revenge on Flynn, as well as Rapunzel and her magic hair.

Meanwhile, Rapunzel, Flynn and Pascal had made it to safety. Rapunzel wrapped her hair round Flynn's injured hand and began to sing. Her glowing hair healed his wound.

When Flynn gathered firewood, Mother Gothel appeared. She wanted to take Rapunzel back to the tower, but Rapunzel refused.

Mother Gothel handed Rapunzel the crown and told her that it was all Flynn wanted. Then she retreated into the forest. Rapunzel wanted to trust Flynn, but she wasn't sure so she hid the crown.

The next morning, Maximus found them but Rapunzel convinced him to let Flynn go just for one day. Suddenly, a bell rang. Rapunzel ran towards it and gasped as she saw the kingdom.

The kingdom was the most exciting thing Rapunzel had ever seen. The people were busy celebrating the birthday of their lost princess.

A group of little girls plaited Rapunzel's locks and pinned them up with flowers. Afterwards, Rapunzel and Flynn joined a crowd as a dance was about to begin.

Suddenly, Rapunzel saw a mosaic behind the stage.
It was of the King and Queen holding a baby girl with
striking green eyes, just like her own.

Rapunzel and Flynn joined
hands and began to dance
around the square.

It was a
wonderful day!

When night fell, Flynn led Rapunzel to a boat and
rowed them to a spot with a perfect view of the kingdom.
Rapunzel gave Flynn the satchel. She was no longer
afraid he would leave once he had the crown.

Beneath the glow of the lanterns, Rapunzel and Flynn held hands and gazed into each other's eyes.

Suddenly, Flynn spotted the Stabbington brothers, so he rowed to land.

Flynn gave the brothers
the crown, but they wanted
Rapunzel! They tied Flynn
to a boat and set him sailing
into the harbour.

Rapunzel saw Flynn sailing away and thought he had betrayed her! She ran into the forest with the brothers in pursuit. Then Rapunzel heard Mother Gothel's voice and found her standing over the unconscious Stabbingtons – Mother Gothel had saved her.

Flynn's boat crashed into a dock. Two guards found him with the stolen crown and put him in prison. Maximus was watching and knew he had to save Flynn and Rapunzel.

In prison, Flynn spotted the Stabbingtons in a cell. They said that Mother Gothel had told them about Rapunzel's hair.

Maximus planned an escape and broke Flynn out of prison. They galloped off to rescue Rapunzel.

Back at the tower, Rapunzel finally realized that she was the lost princess!

Mother Gothel tried to explain, but Rapunzel didn't believe her.

Then Flynn arrived. "Rapunzel! Rapunzel, let down your hair!" he called, and her golden locks fell to the ground.

When Flynn reached the top, he found Rapunzel in chains. Mother Gothel wounded him with a dagger and chained him up, too.

Rapunzel begged to heal Flynn. In return, she promised
to stay with Mother Gothel forever. Mother Gothel
agreed.

Rapunzel placed her hair over Flynn's wound. But he
reached for a piece of broken mirror and cut off her hair!
It turned brown and lost its healing power.

Within moments Mother Gothel aged hundreds of years
and turned to dust!

Rapunzel wept and a golden tear fell upon Flynn's
cheek. The tear glowed and Flynn's entire body glowed,
too. He was healed!

Flynn, Pascal and Maximus reunited Rapunzel with her parents. They all hugged each other tightly, a family once more.

Soon, all of the townspeople gathered for a welcome home party. The King and Queen and the people of the kingdom all released floating lanterns into the sky. The light had guided their princess home at last.

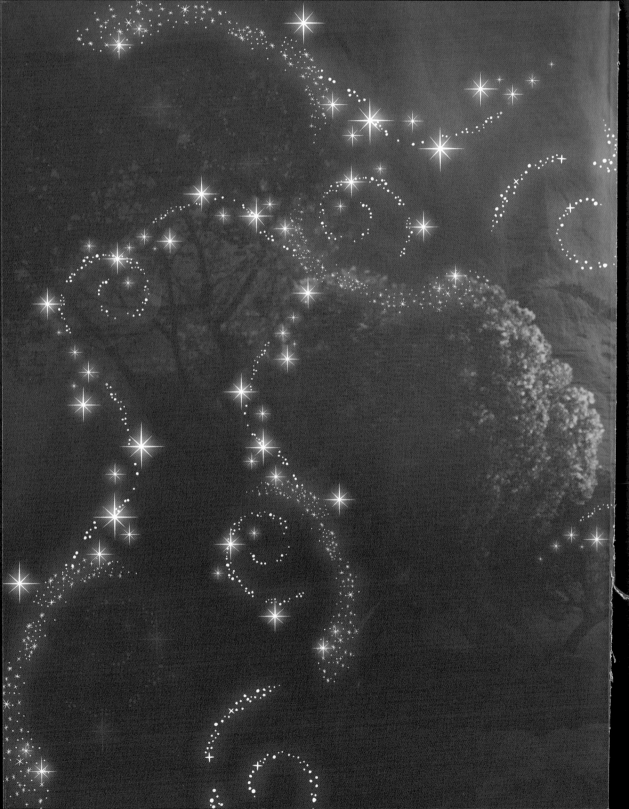